JAKKI WOOD studied graphic design at Wolverhampton Polytechnic.
She has written and illustrated many children's books for Frances Lincoln,
including *Animal Parade, Number Parade, Noisy Parade, Baby Parade,
Bumper to Bumper, The Deep Blue Sea* and *March of the Dinosaurs.*
She lives in Worcestershire.

tipper truck

small dump truck

paver

road roller

road sweeper

A HOLE IN THE ROAD

Jakki Wood

F

FRANCES LINCOLN
CHILDREN'S BOOKS

There is a hole in the road. It needs a new surface.

Workers use a drill to break up the old one.

A backhoe loader is fitted with a big hammer.

This does the job faster.

A mini-excavator makes the hole bigger.

A digger scoops up the rubble.

The rubble is loaded into a dump truck.

Then it is taken away.

A tipper truck brings crushed stones.

The stones fill in the hole.

Hot asphalt arrives in a dump truck.

It is used to make the hard surface of the road.

A paver spreads the hot asphalt…

over the road surface.

A road roller squashes the asphalt flat.

Workers make sure it is really smooth.

A road sweeper cleans the new road…

ready for cars to use again.

mini-excavator

For Isaac Harley Blann and Simeon Harding

First published in Great Britain in 2008 by
Frances Lincoln Children's Books, 4 Torriano Mews,
Torriano Avenue, London NW5 2RZ

www.franceslincoln.com

First paperback edition published in Great Britain in 2009

British Library Cataloguing in Publication Data available on request

ISBN: 978-1-84507-996-3

Printed in Dongguan, Guangdong, China by Toppan Leefung in November 2010

3 5 7 9 8 6 4

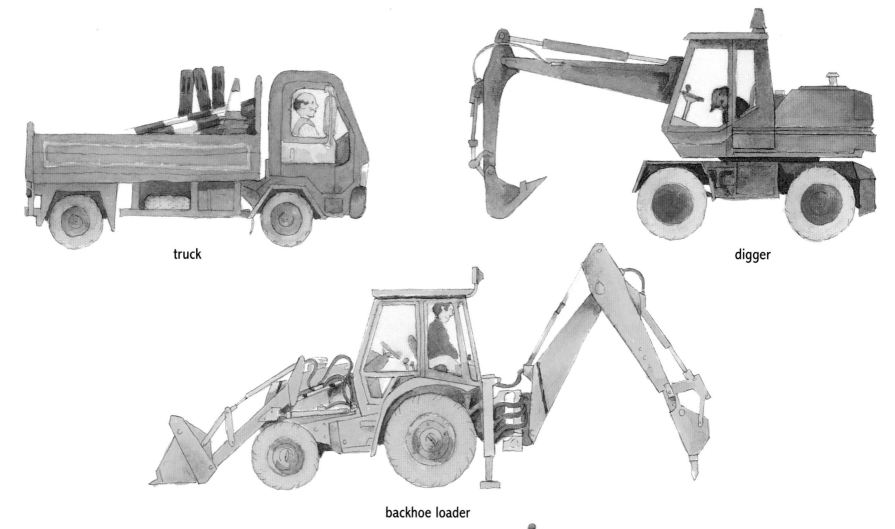

truck

digger

backhoe loader

dump trucks

MORE PAPERBACKS BY JAKKI WOOD
FROM FRANCES LINCOLN CHILDREN'S BOOKS

Bumper to Bumper

Where do you find a sports car, a horsebox, a caravan,
a cement mixer and more than 30 other vehicles all together?
Where else but bumper-to-bumper in a traffic jam? This book
features pictures of vehicles which children can learn
to spot and name.

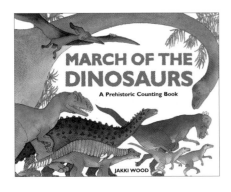

March of the Dinosaurs

From "1 gigantic, huge, colossal ultrasaurus" to "12 busy,
wriggle-tiggle, writhing, squirming, hatching babies", prehistoric
creatures by the dozen slither, hop, and thunder forward in
colourful reptilian parade. Imaginative children and their parents
will find a great deal to talk about in these exciting, vivid pictures
– and a delightful surprise under the pull-out flap at the end.

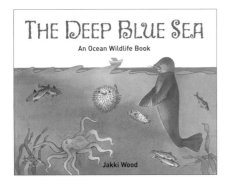

The Deep Blue Sea

A small boy pushes his little boat out to sea to begin a fantastic
adventure travelling all around the world. More than 60 remarkable
ocean creatures (including clownfish, flying fish, anchovies
and whales) swim, dive and glide through the pages of this
sea journey in an informative introduction to ocean creatures.

Frances Lincoln titles are available from all good bookshops.
You can also buy books and find out more about your favourite titles,
authors and illustrators on our website: www.franceslincoln.com